OTHER YOUNG YEARLING BOOKS YOU WILL ENJOY:

PANDA, *Susan Bonners*
THE REAL HOLE, *Beverly Cleary*
TWO DOG BISCUITS, *Beverly Cleary*
JANET'S THINGAMAJIGS, *Beverly Cleary*
THE GROWING-UP FEET, *Beverly Cleary*
THE TREASURE SOCK, *Pat Thomson*
ONE OF THOSE DAYS, *Pat Thomson*
GOOD GIRL GRANNY, *Pat Thomson*
BULLFROG GROWS UP, *Rosamond Dauer*
BULLFROG AND GERTRUDE GO CAMPING,
Rosamond Dauer

YEARLING BOOKS/YOUNG YEARLINGS/YEARLING CLASSICS
are designed especially to entertain and enlighten young
people. Charles F. Reasoner, Professor Emeritus of Children's Literature and Reading, New York University, is
consultant to this series.

For a complete listing of all Yearling titles,
write to Dell Readers Service, P.O. Box 1045,
South Holland, Illinois 60473.

How Santa Claus Had a Long and Difficult Journey Delivering His Presents

BY FERNANDO KRAHN

A YOUNG YEARLING BOOK

Published by
Dell Publishing
a division of
The Bantam Doubleday Dell Publishing Group, Inc.
666 Fifth Avenue
New York, New York 10103

The trademark Yearling® is registered in the U.S. Patent
and Trademark Office.

ISBN: 0-440-40118-6

Reprinted by arrangement with Delacorte Press/
Seymour Lawrence

Printed in the United States of America

December 1988

10 9 8 7 6 5 4 3 2 1

FOR "SAINT" NICHOLAS LAWRENCE

HOW SANTA CLAUS HAD
A LONG AND DIFFICULT JOURNEY
DELIVERING HIS PRESENTS

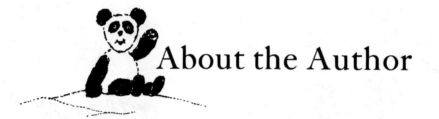

About the Author

FERNANDO KRAHN, artist, cartoonist, and filmmaker, is the creator of many imaginative picture books, some without words, including *Journeys of Sebastian* and *Sebastian and the Mushroom*. He recently illustrated Walt Whitman's classic poem, *I Hear America Singing*. Mr. Krahn was born in Chile and now lives with his wife and children in Spain.